North Pole expr

Ben Hay Expose
Interviewed by
Poppy

Q: How are you today?
A: Very well thank you. How-

Q: Is the tea to your pleasing?
A: Yes, it's perfect. Earl-

Q: I can't help but notice that you cut that last question short?
A: Urmmm...

Q: You aren't trying to hide anything now are you?
A: Poppy?

Q: I'm asking the questions here mister. Did you or did you not write a book?
A: Yes! Yes I did... you got me there...

Q: As I thought. Enough of this chitchat small talk business.
A: ...

Q: Do you Know Sassy and Tumble personally?
A: I've never actually met them. It's quite difficult to get to the North Pole from Oxford where I live most of the time. I haven't passed my driving test yet you see.

Q: How do you stay in touch with Sassy and Tumble?
A: Well, Tumble lets Sassy write most of the letters. Sassy actually owns a typewriter, and can spell. Tumble helps by putting the letters in the letterbox.

Q: How can other adventurers get in touch with you?
A: The North Pole has pretty bad Internet but I do have an email address just in case you don't live there.
You can contact me at:
SassyandTumble@gmail.com

Introduction:

3.5 Billion years ago the first signs of life appear on earth. Subtle and fragile, life is barely noticeable, just a glimmer of what is to come. The young turbulent planet is hostile to all. Powerful volcanoes, vicious storms and earthquakes shape this cruel world.

What hope is there for the little single cell creatures that cower in darkness?

The answer: one brave, clever, acrobatic cell emerges. One adventurous being decides to leave the murky crevasse that it calls home to head north. Its friends and family think this to be madness but wish it luck nonetheless.

This creature braves the worst possible conditions and persists. It grows with each step. Every time lava blocks its path, every time an earthquake splits the very earth before it, it keeps going, and one day reaches the North Pole.

Today Tumble, Sassy and Poppy carry their great ancestors' torch. The adventurous trio fear nothing, know all and will jump at any opportunity to make their mark on history.

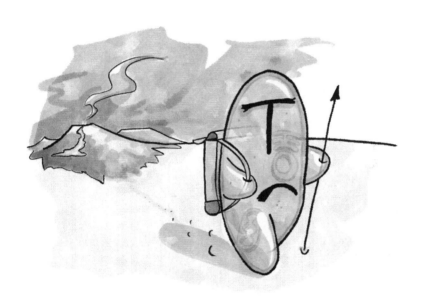

Chapter Selection:

Treasure of the North: Debatably Sassy & Tumble's first real adventure.

Tree Top Rescue: Mr Owlfredo's majestic oak has taken Sassy's cat captive!

Sing Song Sassy: Want to be famous? Sign up to the Talent Show today!

Skate Park: "I feel most alive when I'm carving up the slopes"- Tumble.

Clowning Around: Leo has to watch the crew who are getting up to no good.

Blank Canvas: Good artists copy, great artists steal.

The lost tale of Jackson the penguin farmer: Actions have consequences.

Who Dunnit..?: Was it you? Or you? Sassy is on the case!

Skeletons in the closet: Ghosts are scary, but Tumble is even scarier!

TELEVISION: "Technical difficulties. Please stand by."

School: The epic conclusion. Just a normal day in school really...

THE EXCELLENT ADVENTURES OF SASSY AND TUMBLE

Dedicated to all little adventurers

It was a beautiful May morning on the icy flats of the North Pole. So beautiful in fact that our beloved heroes Sassy and Tumble decided to do some early morning fishing...

"I once caught a fish as big as a small walrus" bragged Tumble. Sassy was watching Tumble as he tried to dislodge a fishing hook from one of his mittens. It had become lodged there when he attempted to tie his famous "Tumble's Knot. The Only True Knot That Does Not Come Undone."

"You know you should really use a Palomar Knot. It won't always come undone and it's really easy to remember," said Sassy.

"The fish was so large that after I managed to drag it back home it fed our family for two whole weeks!" boasted Tumble, after having finally untangled himself from his fishing line, knot still intact.

"I once caught a little fish, no bigger than an acorn, and kept it as a pet. I called it Little Mr. Trawl," said Sassy, with an air of nostalgia to his voice.

"What's an acorn Sassy?" the ever-curious Tumble asked.

"It's a nut belonging to the Fagaceae Family, not often found in the Polar Regions due to-"

"I've got something!" shouted Tumble excitedly.

Out of the water, he proceeded to pull what must surely have been the biggest fish in the ocean. Tumble bravely clenched his mittens around the fishing rod and heaved with all his might. His face was contorted into an expression of pure concentration. Beads of sweat formed on his forehead. With one final tug, and some help from Sassy, he finally got the fish out of the water.

It looked a little bit too shiny to be a fish.

"I think it's a bottle," said Sassy.

"Not a fish?" Tumble poked at it to see whether it was alive. "I think we should get my bow and arrow, just because, you know, it might be dangerous or something". Tumble always used any excuse to use his deadly bow and arrow.

Sassy picked up the bottle, uncorked it, shook it, and out fell a rolled up piece of ancient parchment. He opened it gently, looked at it curiously and said, "It's a map!"

"Careful, it might bite," warned Tumble, examining the mysterious object in Sassy's hand.

"No silly. It shows people where treasures are hidden! You see this cross here in between these letters: *T, O,* & *I, C.* The X always marks the spot where treasure is to be found! You just make the map point north and go there!"

"What does it say at the bottom?" asked Tumble (who knew every single one of the letters of the alphabet but who sometimes, when the sun shone in his eyes or the wind was harsh, couldn't read all that well). Sassy was a better reader anyway, what with him having read all those books and all.

"Dooh... Not drankee. Yes! Definitely Mayan for treasure," said the wise, young Sassy.

"Unimaginable wealth! Maybe some chocolate fudge cake! I have a compass. Let's follow the red arrow to the treasure!" Tumble was terribly excited.

He pointed his compass north, which is difficult when one is already at the North Pole. The needle spun slowly but finally quivered to a stop. He confidently set off in that direction. The scent of adventure was thick in the air. He wondered what they might encounter first... a polar bear? Or maybe pirates?

"Mind our fishing hole!" Sassy warned. But it was too late.

With a little splash Tumble fell face first into the icy water below.

After quickly going home to dry off, and after receiving a telling off from Tumble's mother for being silly, they set off again on their epic journey. Having received ample provisions in the form of biscuits and hot chocolate from Tumble's Mum, they were ready for anything.

They had retraced their footsteps from Tumble's house and soon returned to the nearby fishing hole when Tumble dreamily said,

"You know what? We've been walking for a while now and any famous adventurer would tell you that adventuring isn't really all that much fun on an empty stomach."

"I think I read that in a book once," agreed Sassy, "We should set up camp and eat our provisions".

So Sassy and Tumble unpacked their camping gear and started assembling their trusty tent.

Sassy had once read a one hundred-page book on how to pitch a tent. It was filled with illustrations and many helpful hints. After a little while their masterpiece was complete. They were both very proud of this great achievement. Sassy said it looked just like the ones in his book.

Exhausted after their laborious construction project, they both squeezed into it and eagerly opened their provisions.

Tumble and Sassy ate and talked about what sort of treasure they might find... and about what sort of exciting things they might see... and about what the best sort of biscuit was. They always agreed that Jaffa Cakes were the best.

Sassy knew that technically they weren't actually biscuits at all but kept this as his little secret.

The sun had wandered across the sky and was shining directly down on them by the time they had packed up and continued on their journey.

They had walked for a good ten or eight minutes when they stumbled across a mysterious cave.

"This *must* be where the treasure is hidden," said Tumble. His compass had led them here after all.

"I hope they have some rations," said Sassy. "We seem to have gobbled all of ours up, and we don't want to go hungry again."

Cautiously, they both entered the cave. The stalactites were distorting their shadows in a spooky, kaleidoscopic way. The fearless adventurers nevertheless carefully crept further into the icy mirror maze.

What they saw next surprised them both! Sassy, quick to react, jumped, rolled and hid behind a stalagmite. He took a cautious peek from the safety of his hiding-place. He blinked in disbelief at what he saw.

"Oh! It's only a snowman," said Sassy, realising his cowardly mistake, but Tumble wasn't listening...

Though Tumble had no weapons, he bravely stood his ground.

"Leave me and my friend alone you arctic monster! You mythical creature of purest evil! You'll never take us alive!"

"It's just a snowman Tumble," repeated Sassy, but to no avail.

"Argh!" yelled Tumble and lunged at the snowman, knocking its hat to the ground. Then Tumble balled his fists and exhausted himself by repeatedly punching the heap of snow.

"Are you ok Tumble? It's just snow. I think you can stop now," said the worried Sassy.

Tumble picked up the carrot that served as the snowman's nose and hurled it further into the cave. Now tired and exhausted, Tumble sat triumphantly on a mound of snow, freckled with little mitten marks and said boastfully, "Adventuring is what I do best. Nothing ever scares me! I once fought a polar bear you know. You had nothing to fear Sassy, the situation was under control. I saw this coming from the moment I nearly fatally fell into our fishing hole. An adventurer's sixt-SEVENTH sense if you will. That was exhausting though. Let's go find that treasure and go home".

A howl of wind suddenly rushed through the cave. The sun had nearly sunk below the horizon. The stalactites were jingling menacingly. The two friends looked at each other, both uncertain about whether they wanted to face any other dangers today.

"On the other hand," said Tumble "We have run out of provisions and we don't want to go hungry, and it's getting dark outside."

"We might starve, and we don't want to keep your parents waiting. They always get so worried," agreed Sassy.

So, our two brave heroes decided to call it a day.

They ran out of the cave as quickly as they could and straight back home so they could tell their fantastic tale to their friends and family.

They may not have found any treasure this time but who needs treasure when you have had a really good adventure.

Mrs Tumble had prepared a beautiful breakfast for Tumble; who scoffed his pancakes down in an instant, and swallowed his glass of milk in one hasty gulp.

"You know you'll choke one day if you don't eat more slowly," scolded Mrs Tumble.

"Nonsense, you need to eat quickly so that you can... *cough*... do more fun things during the day," protested the red-faced Tumble.

His mother sighed. "Run along now and make sure you don't get into trouble young boy," she said and nudged Tumble out of the door.

Tumble looked around. Fresh snow lay everywhere. He picked some up, squeezed it into a perfect ball, and judged its structural integrity to be well suited for fun. He imagined building the biggest snow fort in the world.

"Tumble!" called an agitated voice.

It was Sassy! He was running around the corner of Tumble's street; out of breath and in obvious haste.

"What's the matter Sassy?" asked Tumble, who was in the middle of weighing up his snowball. He decided that this particular one was calibrated to be thrown expertly at a lamp post, or a fence, or even a letterbox... He was the best snowball thrower that he knew.

"My cat, King Cole has disappeared! I can't find her anywhere!"

Out of shock, Tumble let go of the snowball, mid-throw!

The two delinquents watched as it sailed over the neighbours' houses and far into the street beyond.

It landed with a dramatic "Thunk!" which was followed by a sensational "Splat!" and presumably came to rest as a surprised "OW!?" completed the frozen spheroid's parabolic journey. A voice could be heard complaining that the weather really had taken a turn for the worse, what with these snowball showers and all...

After having recovered their breath from rushing off, the two friends discussed how they could find King Cole.

"It's not easy because she is completely white, except for her nose..." said Sassy.

"Yes," agreed Tumble.

"And because we live on the North Pole, it might be hard to see her..." continued Sassy.

"Mm-hmm," agreed Tumble with a slight scratch of his chin.

"Because the North Pole is also mostly white," concluded Sassy.

"Ah yes, very clever of you Sassy. You cannot see white on white. We should therefore look somewhere that isn't white... Like a tree... Or a volcano," the deductive Tumble added.

It turned out that Sassy knew a lot about trees, because he had many books in his igloo. He also knew that Mr Owlfredo lived in one.

Mr Owlfredo was a person who enjoyed telling off Tumble, Sassy and their friends when they played ice hockey on the frozen lake that lay in front of his tree-top home. He would yell at them out of one of his little broken windows and to add insult to injury, regularly told their parents how naughty they all had been.

You naughty kids!

Tumble and Sassy knew that they would have to proceed with extreme caution, if they didn't want to get told off.

They set off with determination and after a short walk arrived at Mr. Owlfredo's grand tree with a house built in it.

"King Cole!" bellowed Tumble and Sassy. "King Cole! Where are you?"

An answer came in the form of a "Meow" from far above them.

Sassy and Tumble looked up.

King Cole's little face was poking over the roof of Mr Owlfredo's house.

"How did she get up there?" wondered Sassy out loud.

"How is she going to get back down?" asked Tumble.

They discussed their possible options. Knocking on old Owlfredo's door was out of the question because he might of course be asleep or have a guest around.

They were not at all scared of Mr. Owlfredo but they agreed it would be rude to disturb him. They were going to have to use all of their combined brainpower and imagination to come up with a solution to the problem of getting King Cole down from the roof.

They both thought hard....

And thought some more...

After some tense moments Sassy suggested getting a ladder from the fire department. Sassy knew for a fact that they always had ladders to cut down the highest tree branches, which were very scarce in the desolate snowy wilderness. These tree branches were then burnt as fuel to heat the people's houses. Hence-

Tumble stopped Sassy before he finished his explanation.

Time was of utmost importance if they were going to get cat King Cole down before she was noticed by the wicked Mr. Owlfredo.

So off they went...

The two had gotten their ladder, some hot chocolate and an informative talk on fire safety before returning to Mr. Owlfredo's house not 2 hours later.

"King Cole, I'm coming! Hold the ladder Tumble. Quick! I'm going up..."

Tumble reached up as high as he could and firmly held the first rung of the ladder so that Sassy wouldn't fall. Sassy cautiously inched his way to the top.

Then suddenly!

"Hey, you pesky robbers!" yelled Mr. Owlfredo, who had leapt to the window just as Sassy neared the top of the ladder.

"Get off my tree house you thieves! You will never get your mittens on my precious stamp collection, so don't even try!"

"We just want our cat back. PLEASE!!" begged Sassy.

"That's exactly what someone who wants my stamps would say!" yelled Mr Owlfredo. He must have thought that the boys were *cat* burglars...

"Tumble! King Cole! Help! Help!" sobbed Sassy as Mr. Owlfredo started to shake the ladder viciously.

Tumble was trying as best he could to hold on to the bottom rung so that Sassy wouldn't fall. But try as he might he could not hold on for much longer. His grip started to weaken, and then his mittens slipped off the bottom rung.

"Heeeeeeelllllpppp, Crunch!" yelped Sassy as he fell off the ladder and plopped into a gigantic heap of snow.

They were going to have to try something else...

After returning the ladder to the fire brigade, they again thought of ways of getting King Cole down from Mr. Owlfredo's roof.

"What we should try to do is to encourage King Cole to come down by herself," suggested Sassy.

"Yes. It's definitely easier to go down a tree than it is to go up one," said Tumble, remembering Sassy's hasty descent.

"We just need a way to let King Cole land safely on her feet, without scaring her... Wait... A... Minute...The circus is in town! We could use one of their trapeze safety trampolines! They always have a trapeze safety trampoline so that if the show gets too boring, they can throw in a couple of bounces to liven things up!"

Sassy had obviously had a great idea, but Tumble couldn't figure out what it was. Did he want the trapeze performers to bounce all the way up the tree and grab King Cole? Yes! That was clever! They could jump up and...

"And then the clowns could tell jokes and King Cole wouldn't be so scared! We could get our pal Poppy along too. She's always up for adventuring"

"Let's goooo!" said Sassy urgently.

And off they went again…

They returned a while later with a small, round trampoline.

"It's a shame there was a show on. I think the trapeze artists would have enjoyed saving King Cole, and Poppy could have used her lion-taming skills to teach King Cole some new tricks," said Tumble.

"Maybe we can just tell them about it later and not leave out a single detail. Then it's nearly like they were here with us," said Sassy, who knew that people were going to want to hear about this fantastic tale.

So Sassy carefully placed the red and yellow trampoline under the northern side of Mr. Owlfredo's ancient, rickety, polar oak tree; a botanic specimen unique to Tumble and Sassy's town.

And then they waited. And waited. But King Cole did not leap from the tree…

"I am going to have to show her how it is done, so that she can learn from me," said Tumble, having thought through every other rational option for coaxing King Cole down.

So, they moved the trampoline to a smaller nearby tree and Tumble, after a couple of stretches, climbed to the very top.

"Okay King Cole, you don't have to look down, you simply have to make sure you land on your feet. The trampoline will cushion your fall. Just like this!"

Tumble gracefully fell through the air and then less gracefully landed on the trampoline, which made a "POING!" sound and catapulted Tumble straight into a gigantic heap of snow.

They were going to have to try something else...

Our heroes were getting tired and were fast running out of ideas.

Sassy, in a moment of near cosmic enlightenment remembered something about Mr. Owlfredo. Something that might help them save King Cole.

He turned to Tumble and spoke in a hushed tone. "Rumour has it that Mr. Owlfredo never wanted to live in a tree house, he simply dropped a seed in the ground when he built the house and over the years, as the tree grew, it lifted the house into the air," Tumble digested this information carefully; examining the new facts with delicate deliberation.

"So... if we managed to get King Cole out of the tree and at the same time managed to get old Owlfredo's house back to the ground, where it should be, we would be doing everyone a great favour." said Tumble. "Wait here!".

Tumble came back two and a bit minutes later with one of his father's wood-saws, and gave it to Sassy.

Sassy knew exactly what Tumble had in mind.

"OK. All we have to do is cut the tree at an angle, like this," said Sassy and enthusiastically began to demonstrate by cutting at the tree's ancient roots.

"And gravity will make the tree fall into the frozen lake, breaking the ice, and because the house is made of wood and is therefore buoyant, it will float!"

"Picture a floating house! Who wouldn't want one of those?" agreed the imaginative Tumble.

They took a saw-handle each and started cutting at the tree trunk.

Up in the house Mr. Owlfredo awoke from his midday nap. He couldn't help but notice that his bed and chandelier were slowly swaying from side to side. He went to his balcony in a confused haze and was shocked to see Tumble and Sassy making quick work of his precious tree trunk.

"YOU KIDS THERE! GET AWAY FROM MY HOUSE!", he shrieked angrily. Frightened, Tumble and Sassy jumped into the air!

Scared for their lives they ran all the way home before Mr. Owlfredo could tell them off properly.

...

That evening, Mr. Owlfredo did complain to Tumbles Parents. The mean old man!

Then Tumble and Sassy both got a huge telling off from Tumble's mother for being silly and were sent to bed.

The tree house sadly never actually fell into the lake to become an awesome floating house and luckily no one was really hurt.

No one apart from Sassy, who still hadn't gotten his beloved cat back. He crept into bed with a heavy heart and fell asleep sad.

As if by a miracle, in the middle of the night, the cat flap of Sassy's igloo opened, and a pair of feathered hands pushed an exhausted King Cole through.

She went straight to the sleeping Sassy and cuddled up next to him. How happy he would be in the morning.

Mr. Owlfredo scuttled off into the night, as the full moon began to disappear behind a lonely cloud.

Sassy and Tumble were sitting on a park bench just watching the Northpolian people go about their lives. It was a beautiful day and our two heroes were in a creative mood.

"Did you know it's our school talent show tomorrow?" asked Tumble, who for the past three years had come second, third and fifth chronologically with his hilarious impersonations of their head teacher, Principal Dimly. "We need something that will really impress the judges this year."

"The winners always seem to be singers," pointed out Sassy, "We should sing a song."

The two looked up at the clouds and imagined their futures as famous musicians.

In the daydream, Tumble was a world-renowned drummer, who performed wearing a blindfold and played to his whole entire hometown. Lasers and fireworks would be his trademark, and everyone would love his original beats.

Sassy by contrast was a monocled jazz trumpeter who was never appreciated by his townsfolk, but who with persistence became a famous composer and set up his own School of Jazz in a far away land...

They both knew that the winners would receive the prestigious "Cup of Talent" (C of T for short).

They were going to have to create a very good song to guarantee a win.

"I'm going to set a beat" said Tumble spontaneously and proceeded to rhythmically hit the park-bench with his mittens.

"Boom, boom, boom, bit bap ski bop ha-braap braap ikki ikki skiwiki," sang the jolly Tumble.

Sassy looked on, impressed with Tumble's obvious musical talent.

After taking a moment to appreciate his friend's musical prowess, and getting in touch with the beat, Sassy sang the following in a silky-smooth voice:

"Teachers really should vote for us.
All the other acts that follow us.
Will not be as good as us.
So don't create a -um- fuss.
Just vote for us!"

"-hip skip hip hoola hoop..."

"We are not doing it for the fame,
And we are not the... same."
We... have...um...
So vote for us!"

Sassy made a mental note to buy a book of rhyming words on his way home.

Sassy and Tumble looked at each other. They knew that what had just been created must be amongst the greatest musical achievements of their generation. Classy Sassy and Rumble Tumble, the greatest musical double act of all time had been born.

"We are bound to win!" proclaimed Sassy cheerily.

"I'm going to go home to write some really good lyrics for our act. We can just improvise the rest on stage I reckon. We should probably wear some great costumes as well!" and with that our two heroes went their separate ways.

Tumble arrived at his house shortly afterwards. He knew that he would have to practise a lot over the next few hours to become the best drummer in the world. He politely asked his mother for some pots and pans and exhausted himself by creating some incredible beats. The sweaty Tumble came into the kitchen for a refreshing glass of milk.

"Tumble, what are you doing in the living room? If you want to get some exercise you could just go for a run and not make such a racket," said Tumble's mother.

"I'm not exercising Mum. I'm creating great beats for the school talent show tomorrow." Tumble's mother did not look convinced. "Sassy and I are doing a musical act. We are bound to win the C of T this year, I just need to keep practising hard. Oh, and if you have one, I just need a costume of some sort as well"

Tumble's mother had a sympathetic-yet-mischievous smile on her face. "Well honey, I wish you the best of luck. I can give you a suit to wear for tomorrow."

Tumble reluctantly tried on the white suit.

His mother reassured him that he looked very handsome. Tumble had seen himself as more of a musical cowboy or a dragon, but there was no arguing with his mother.

The morning of the competition arrived. Tumble, his mother and Sassy were sitting at the back of the School hall watching the other acts. Personally, Sassy thought that they lacked finesse - or whatever the word he had looked up that morning and painstakingly memorized was. The judges were looking very impressed.

"She's rather good," said Tumble's mother, enjoying the closing acrobatic stunts of their friend Poppy.

Wait till they see us, thought Tumble.

"I thought she lacked... fins," said Sassy. His entire face beamed with pride. He knew that clever words impressed people.

A comedy troupe and a tap dancer followed. Finally their friend Poppy returned a second time with her pet lion after a plea for an encore. This time though the latter never got to start her act because the audience protested about lions being dangerous, or something. Sassy and Tumble were very sad about this. Poppy nearly always kept Leo under control.

"Up next... um..."Classy Sassy and Rumble Tumble. The greatest musical duo of our time," read Mrs Appleshine from a card.

Up the two musicians went, they bowed clumsily and started to play.

"Boom, boom, crashhhhhh, booom tap tap crashhhhh tap boom!" went Tumble's drum set.

Sassy, bobbing to the beat, raised his head with a stern expression and started to sing...

"We love music more than anything. So much so that we want to win"

"Tap, ratatat tap, crash" Tumble was in his element.

Sassy had read a book on subliminal messaging the night before and knew that by putting enough subtle self-praising lyrics into his song, the judges were going to vote for the duo subconsciously. He sang the following:

"The flowers grow at all hours," followed by a quick and quiet *"*So vote for us*"*

The sun shines above the clouds when the weather is dull,
We are the best
We ride the stormy waves like a boat's hull,
Vote Classy Sassy and Rumble Tumble... we are the best act... honest"
Sassy mimicked a boat cresting a wave, with a thumbs up as a mast, and winked at the judges from behind his sunglasses.

"Tap tap boing, scratch scratch..."

"Boing scratch!"

In Sassy's mind the judges' eyes were hypnotised swirls, every one of his subtle messages would be persuading them to give the musical duo a higher score. The judges' glazed over expressions and thoughtful slouches were all signs that Sassy's genius techniques were working perfectly. Like puppets on a string, he thought.

"... So with no further ado, here are the two,
vote Sassy!
Best musicians in the whole of North Pole City!
Make no mistake, vote for us"

"Crash   boom   boom   tap   tap,   tap...
tap.........boom.....tap..........."

Our heroes remained on stage, waiting for the well-deserved onslaught of applause.

"Tappp............"

The judges looked on. The parents (after an awkward hesitation) started clapping politely.

"They loved us Sassy!" said Tumble, poking his head over the drum kit. "We *are* going to win!"

The two walked off stage, smug as can be. More acts followed: a ventriloquist, a juggler and even an impressionist, but Sassy and Tumble paid no heed. They knew there was no real competition.

The time to announce the winners had finally come. The hall fell silent. Everyone held their breath as principal Dimly opened the winner's envelope...

"Ahem. Ladies and gentlemen, boys and girls, the winner of this year's talent competition is... Mr. Button McShane for his hilarious impression of none other than myself! Well done Button, come onto the stage you champ and receive your trophy. The prestigious Cup of Talent!"

After what our two musicians thought was way too much applause for an act that Tumble had basically invented, they sulked home.

"Button did do a great impression," said Tumble with a tiny quiver in his voice. "Only really *I* could have outdone him. He had the voice all wrong and wasn't nearly tall enough..."

"A great show like ours can change the world though Tumble, you know. I think we really stirred some souls today." said Sassy encouragingly. Tumble nodded weakly.

They both turned without really saying goodbye. They needed some time apart for once. For now, they parted ways.

The crisp arctic air was all that kept Sassy company as he sulked home. Without really meaning to he started thinking.   He was sure that he must have touched at least a couple of souls today because subliminal messaging was an exact science after all. Books didn't lie! Sassy was sure that he had mastered the techniques from this book because he had spent ages practicing them on Cat King Cole. So long in fact that he hardly had any time to write lyrics or to create a costume.

He whistled the song to himself. It wasn't all that bad, was it? He would have voted for himself, he knew that much. And so would have Tumble...

So, in a way, he had in fact stirred some souls! The subliminal techniques had worked! Albeit only on the two of them.

It was only a little victory, but made him feel better.

Relieved, Sassy quickened his pace and headed home to feed his cat. Maybe he would treat her to a rendition of the song as well. Every vote counted after all.

So, our two beloved heroes may not have won the competition this time around, but they did perform a great show (though much under-appreciated in their own time) and entertained the school for a whole three minutes.

And in the end that was all that really mattered to them.

Not the fame, nor the fortune nor the Cup of Talent.

Just taking part was enough.

There would always be next year...

It had snowed a great deal over the past couple of days. Now the whole town was covered in a soft fluffy blanket, perfect weather for going to the snowboard park.

Tumble had taken his father's old snowboard out of the tool shed and was looking forward to inventing some new tricks on the slopes. Maybe even breaking a record or two...

"Honey, where do you think you are going? Take your sister with you. I have to do some shopping so you are in charge of babysitting for the day," called Tumble's mother from the living room.

How did she always know when he was leaving the house? No matter how sneaky he was, she always knew. She must have x-ray vision or maybe she was a trained spy...

"And don't you think that a snowboard is a little dangerous? Take a toboggan instead. It's safer and you won't hurt anyone."

"Ok Mum. Will do" sighed Tumble and went to get his toboggan and his baby sister, Kate.

He pulled the toboggan through town to the ski slopes with little Kate happily sitting on top of it. All the kids from school were there. Everyone was whizzing about on snowboards and skis. Sassy was at the bottom of the slope building a huge ramp.

It must have been the biggest ramp ever built by Sassy, who was the resident expert ramp-builder, and it looked like everyone was eager to test it out.

Sassy looked up the slope and said, "Ok Button, it's ready! Just make sure you hit it at exactly the right angle. Otherwise you might fly off and hit those trees over there and experience a lethal entropic increase!"

"OK! Here goes!" shouted their dare devil friend Button and pushed off.

He was building up ludicrous speed. He was nothing more than an orange blur. Everyone held their breath as he neared the ramp. Button hit it perfectly and whirled through the air, landing some 15 meters away. Everyone was stunned!
That took a real expert to pull off! Tumble knew he was going to have to put in some real effort to beat it.

He walked over to Sassy. They greeted each other with their secret handshake, had an in-depth conversation about nunchucks and admired Tumble's toboggan whilst discussing whether painting flames on it would make it go faster. Finally, Tumble explained that he was going to attempt to beat Button's jump.

"Are you mad Tumble?! That was an impossible jump, and you've only ever really done stunts on your toboggan!"

Tumble was insistent though and convinced Sassy to teach him how to become an expert snowboarder. Sassy had of course read many books on snowboarding and ramp-building and was the perfect teacher for Tumble. They pulled Kate, the toboggan and a snowboard up the hill and examined the task at hand. The ramp did look pretty big from up there.

Sassy inspected the slope, rubbed his chin, put his finger in the air as if he was measuring the wind, drew a picture in the snow with numbers on it, squinted at the sun and confidently nodded to himself.

"You should be fine. I mean, you have crosswinds and turbulence and you're going pretty fast, but you basically just have to make a perfect run. That's the secret! As someone who has read books on the subject, I can safely say that being really good at snowboarding is the key." Sassy nodded sagely for effect. Then he continued "The challenge, really, is not making any mistakes. As long as you don't make any mistakes you should really be fine. No biggie."

"Thanks Sassy! I reckon I could make it a bit more exciting, maybe throw in a backflip or do it wearing a blindfold or whatever", said Tumble eagerly.

Tumble strapped himself to the snowboard, fell over, got back up, got Sassy to clumsily push him to the edge of the slope, and prepared himself for his greatest stunt to date.

Tumble looked a little anxious.

"You really helped me there. I don't think I could do this without you as my teacher Sassy. Thanks buddy." Tumble was confident that with Sassy's advice everything would be fine.

Here goes...

Just as Tumble was about to push off, Sassy noticed Kate, forgotten on her toboggan, slowly slipping down the slope. Tumble and Sassy watched, frozen to the spot. Kate's toboggan was building up speed. Tumble's mouth dropped open in awe. Sassy could only point. Kate was heading straight for the ramp! She had to be saved before it was too late! Sassy knew he would have to react quickly to save her!

"We have to do something. Now!" screamed Sassy urgently and shoved Tumble down the hill.

"Arrrrrrrrrahawaaaahrrrrgh!" was all Tumble could say in protest.

He was now racing down the slope, hot on the heels of his baby sister. He decided to stop screaming, squinted his eyes slightly and focused hard on his sister, who was sprawled on the speeding toboggan. He could catch up with her! He knew he could!

The ramp was looming rapidly. Tumble remembered Sassy's advice:

Be like the wind Tumble...

He concentrated harder than he ever had before. He had to save Kate! He was the bloomin' babysitter after all!!!

The toboggan and Kate flew over the edge of the ramp.

Tumble followed, and with what can only be described as a miracle, caught Kate in mid air. He hugged Kate tightly to himself, somehow did a forward flip, and perfectly landed his jump.

Kate was saved!

Everyone on the slope looked at Tumble and marvelled at what he had just done. No one had ever seen such an incredible stunt...

After much fuss over Tumble and Kate everyone decided that Tumble was indeed the greatest snowboarder on the slopes. Sassy was answering questions about his teaching techniques and Tumble was saying that snowboarding ran in the family, and that Kate was going to learn from the very best.

Button came over and said, "Tumble, that was incredible! You must be the best snowboarder in history! How did you do that?"

"Well" answered Tumble "The secret is being a natural, and drinking two glasses of milk every day. Obviously, that's really all it takes. I can honestly do a lot better. Yeah, honest. I have even invented my very own trick: 'The Flight of the Tumble-Bee'. That's what I call it. I made that up myself. If you want to see it, I could give you a quick demonstration".

Everyone was terribly keen. Tumble was having the time of his life. After signing some autographs in the snow he got back into position.

He already knew what 'The Flight of the Tumble-Bee' would be.

He had been conceiving this trick for weeks now. Meticulously choreographing every step.

He would do a quadruple backflip. He looked down the slope. It suddenly looked like a sheer drop...

...

People who witnessed what happened next all agree that Tumble was very brave for attempting such a dangerous and impossible trick. They also agreed that "The Flailing Tumble" (that's what it came to be called) could have been the best trick ever.
Many people visited little Tumble in hospital, and signed his many, many casts.

Button even took all the pieces of the historic snowboard that had been used and got them put back together in case Tumble ever attempt the trick again.

Poppy sent him a heartfelt circus-themed get-well-soon card and promised that she would teach him how to fall properly without hurting himself (once he had recovered).

Sassy did all of Tumble's homework (as usual) and kept him company.

Tumble knew that he would have to get some more lessons from Sassy before attempting 'The Flight of the Tumble-Bee' again.

They would also have to work on making the trick more exciting, as people knew what to expect now.

But for the time being he was just happy that Kate was safe.

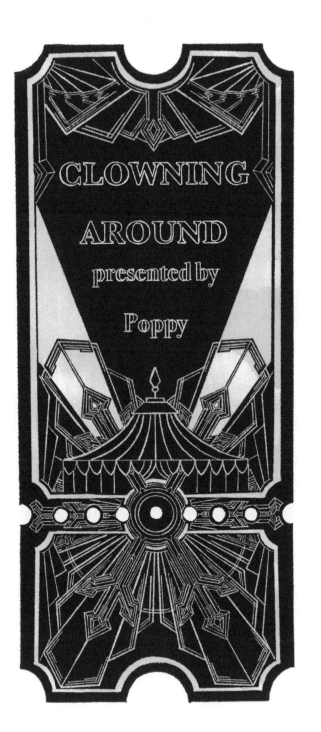

The circus was in town again after a pole-wide winter tour. Poppy had given Sassy and Tumble tickets to the performance and our two restless onlookers were sitting in the crowd, eagerly awaiting the show.

The lights dimmed. The ringmaster stepped into the grand circle and with a wave of his hand silenced the crowd. Sassy and Tumble could hardly contain themselves.

The ringmaster announced, "Our first act of the evening, Ladies and Gentlemen, is a daring feat of bravery and wit. Please welcome to the stage Poppy and her ferocious lion, Leo!"

The crowd fell silent. A single spotlight fell on Poppy in her leotard. A huge lion was circling her slowly and growling menacingly. Poppy confidently held up a hula-hoop and beckoned for the lion to jump through it. The lion confidently planted his feet. He snarled and showed his dagger-like teeth. He coiled like a snake, preparing to lunge at little Poppy.

And then...

He jumped!

Tumble didn't actually see the rest of the brilliant act, for he had fainted. He woke up with Poppy and Sassy looking down over him. They had to explain to him that he had passed out, and that he had to be dragged to Poppy's trailer to get some rest.

"I don't think I really fully fainted," said Tumble quietly, and then even more quietly. "The excitement must have gotten to me or something". But no one was listening, for Poppy was in deep conversation with Sassy.

"The act has to be more exciting Sassy! We need to give the audience exactly what they want. I know I can do better."

"Maybe I can help you create your act," said Sassy shyly. Poppy thought this was a great idea.

Tumble, not to be outdone, dizzily rolled out of bed and joined the conversation.

"Ummmmm. I think, that, the act... could maybe be more exciting too. You may have noticed that I actually genuinely fell asleep during that last performance..."

Poppy and Sassy both looked at Tumble sympathetically.

Everyone agreed that a new act should be created.

Tumble was quick off the mark and suggested setting fire to the hula-hoop. Poppy seemed impressed with that idea.

Sassy parried and put forward an idea involving setting Leo on fire. Poppy thought that was a good idea too (as long as Leo wore a flameproof suit).

So then Tumble, to up the ante, thought that maybe three sharks could replace Leo the lion. Poppy didn't like that idea one bit! Leo was her lifelong friend after all and took part in all of her shows.

Sassy chimed in. Maybe Poppy could jump through a hoop held in Leo's mouth. That was the best idea yet!

(Even Leo thought that was a good idea.)

So Sassy and Poppy talked about their act, and about how lions were the best animals, and how sharks were overrated.

Tumble would have to play to his strengths if he wanted to be involved. He interrupted their conversation by saying the following:

"What you really need is for someone who is brave and fearless to be part of your act"

After a pensive moment, Poppy said, "That's genius Tumble! But who do we know who is brave and fearless..." she tapped her chin thoughtfully.

Tumble stood tall. Chest out, gazing into the middle distance. A silhouette of purest bravery.

"Hmm, maybe, you could perform in the act Tumble?"

Tumble let out a long, exasperated breath which he had been holding in for the entirety of Poppy's drawn out selection process.

"Pfwuuuuuuuuuuuuuuuuuuuuuuuuuh... If you insist Poppy. I will do it. Just for you." What a gentleman he was. She had fallen straight into his trap.

Poppy liked the idea of including her tiny blue canon-ball shaped friend in her performance. She saw how sad Sassy looked at the thought of not being part of the act though.

"Don't worry Sassy, you can help me choreograph the act! Come on. Let's get to work. Bye-bye Tumble, we'll see you next week for your big debut! This is going to be so much fun!"

As Poppy turned to leave, Tumble could have sworn that he saw the faintest hint of a cheeky little smile on her face.

Everyone was terribly exited. Tumble went home chuffed as can be for being chosen for his bravery. He always thought that maybe he was destined to be in the circus.

Sassy and Poppy worked hard on the most daring act of all time and Leo did some household chores.

What could possibly go wrong?

Nothing much happened that week. Sassy and Poppy kept working on the act. Tumble got into a little bit of trouble here and there but nothing to worry yourselves about dear reader.

Finally, the day arrived. Tumble's first ever circus performance. How exciting! Should he perhaps have asked the others what the act was and maybe have practiced a bit? No. He was sure it would all be fine. His bravery was all that he needed.

He met Sassy and Poppy backstage. Poppy asked him whether he was nervous. "NOooOo!" he exclaimed.

Should he be, he briefly wondered? Too late. No time to ask questions. The lights dimmed and the performance was about to start.

"Just stand on that cross marked on the floor Tumble," said Sassy.

"Break a leg," whispered Poppy into Tumble's ear.

Wait! What? Tumble asked himself. He was shoved out from behind the curtain and stumbled into to the ring.

The spotlight was on him. He awkwardly walked over to the cross and realised he was standing in front on a huge red and white target.

He was suddenly very unsure about his recent life choices. He should really have gone back and finished cutting down Mr. Owlfredo's tree. Why did he decide to become a world-class adventurer instead of becoming a drummer? Couldn't he be both? He couldn't go back now though. It was too late. His friends depended on him.

"Ladies and gentlemen, Poppy!" said a voice, and the crowd started cheering as Poppy appeared at the edge of the stage.

Poppy walked into the light and held in her one hand three glistening daggers. Gulp. In the other hand she held a blindfold.

She securely blindfolded herself and addressed the crowd.

"What you are about to witness has never been attempted in the Arctic before. This act is daring and exciting. If you are squeamish, divert your eyes! I will throw these daggers at fearless Tumble!"

The crowd was astounded. She got Leo to point her vaguely in the right direction. Then, without hesitation, threw a dagger between Tumble's legs. Tumble was white as a sheet. THUD...THUD... went the other two daggers and the room went black.

Tumble had fainted again: the poor soul.

Sassy, Poppy and Leo were leaning over him again.

Sassy was apologising for being so reckless in creating the act, and Poppy was just happy that Tumble hadn't hurt himself when he fell.

"Ok Tumble, you were very brave but maybe the circus isn't for you," said Poppy earnestly.

"Nonsense! Personally, I still think the act needs sharks involved somehow," replied Tumble hazily.

Sassy put a friendly hand on Tumble's shoulder, and said "Let's go home buddy, you did great."

They all agreed that the act was a success but that maybe Poppy, who was trained, was the only one who should be performing in a circus.

Sassy said goodbye to Poppy and lead Tumble home.

"You did real good buddy. Yea real good. Honestly buddy you did really real-" Sassy's voice faded as he gently guided Tumble in the direction of home.

...

Poppy sat alone in her trailer that evening. The rhythmic hail beating down on the cold tin roof above her head got her thinking.

She wondered whether she had asked too much of Tumble. He was the bravest person she knew for sure, but maybe they had taken it a step too far this time.

It was true though, thought Poppy, that the act would have been improved if sharks had been involved somehow.

And maybe if Tumble had been a little bit on fire...

A recent blizzard had lifted, and the townsfolk of North Pole City were going about clearing up after the storm. This meant that the children got a snow-day off school.

None of the teachers could leave their houses because the snow-covered roads made it perilously dangerous to drive.

That morning a letter was delivered to Tumble's house by owl post, telling the parents that the children were nevertheless expected to do schoolwork from home. Before his trusting parents drove to work that morning, Tumble assured them that he would work hard all day long. Home alone, he quickly got bored with throwing snowballs at the neighbour's satellite dish though and called Sassy to see whether he wanted to go on an adventure.

"I really ought to do homework, Tumble, so I can't really go adventuring today, but maybe you could come over and we could work together," said Sassy, engrossed in a comic book about time-travelling cannibals. That sounded like a great idea...

A short while later, our two heroes were making the best use of their time by foraging around in the local skip.

All sorts of things can be learnt in skips.

"Look what I found!" burst out Sassy.

Tumble's head inquisitively popped out from a box of old coins.

"What is it?" asked Tumble.

"Oh, this old thing? It's an easel. The word comes from the old German for donkey. It is used by artists to paint on."

Sassy had obviously been reading that book on world facts, which he had bought before the school quiz last week.

"And look, there is a box of art supplies, right next to that antique grandfather clock." Tumble noticed.

He carefully climbed over a rickety old grand piano, accidentally playing a catchy little jingle, and picked up the discarded supplies. He returned, a little green, for one of the paint buckets had split open, covering his coat and mittens.

"Here. Let's get creative. Now we just need something to paint on"

Sassy, as a natural artist, thought that Tumble already looked like an abstract work of art but kept his critique to himself.

They scoured the landscape for something suitable. Sassy, with hands cupped over his eyes to mimic binoculars, spotted a flat rectangle of not 3 feet from him. It was perfect for painting! He picked it up and examined it.

"This should do. It's a bit of a shame that it's been scribbled on though."

"Look here in the corner" said Tumble. "It's a name: Jackson P-. Hmmm. It must be Jackson the Penguin farmer! Can we paint over it?"

"It might hurt his feelings," answered the affectionate Sassy.

The dilemma resolved itself naturally when they accidentally placed a bucket of white paint hazardously close to the edge of a container, and accidentally tipped the paint all over the painting. It took a couple of shoves, but the fatal mistake had been made.

"OH NO!" They both said in unison.

"How silly of us... Let's paint!" enthused Tumble, brush already in hand.

They both took inspiration from what was around them: the twisted metal pipes of an old organ, the faded colours of derelict cars, the metallic shine of that safe over there. They painted vigorously. When they were finished they both took a step back and admired their work. It was magnificent. The bottom, mostly painted by Tumble, and the top exclusively by Sassy both looked fantastic.

"I think you should sign it Sassy. You know more about art than I do,"

"Really? Thanks buddy. We'll split the earnings though. I reckon this could earn up to... say... £20." Said Sassy.

"£20!" Repeated Tumble.

"Maybe £22. It is a masterpiece after all," said Sassy.

They decided to go to the local art fair that weekend to sell their painting. They were going to be rich beyond belief!

Tumble could finally buy that miniature demolition kit he had always wanted.

The weekend rolled around and our two artists woke bright and early to get a good spot at the fair. They proudly exhibited their art amongst all the other pieces. Some were rather good, but nothing came close to capturing the imagination of the onlookers quite like Sassy and Tumble's piece.

Tumble was telling potential customers the dramatic story of how it had been conceived. It had come to Sassy in a dream... It portrayed much more than was revealed at first glance... One had to look past the picture, not at the picture... They all seemed impressed, before sympathetically wishing them the best of luck and hurrying away.

It was early afternoon and business was going rather well.

"Hey Sassy, hey Sonny-Jim-Bob! How're you doing?" It was Tumble's Dad. "What are you guys doing here?"

"We are selling a work of art, and, just between the two of us, Dad, it is a priceless masterpiece," whispered Tumble.

"Wow, no way! Is this it? Did you draw this Sassy? It's incredible! Oh... what? It's this one? I... Um. I love it!" Said Tumble's ever enthusiastic Dad.

He always thought that encouraging the boys to do something that did not involve property damage was a good idea.

Sassy looked very proud of himself. "Thank you. Tumble actually helped me a bit too."

"I can tell!" said Tumble's Dad. "What are you calling it?"

"Um, do I need to give it a name?" asked Sassy.
"If I give it a name I'll become attached to it and then I wouldn't be able to sell it."

Tumble's Dad replied, "I guess I will have to name it then. 'Art School Participation Award' seems like a good name. How much are you two cutthroats asking for it?"

Sassy and Tumble huddled and discussed the issue in hushed whispers. "... But, it's a masterpiece!...", "...Look at the composition!...", "...it has a bloomin' dinosaur!... They turned back to Tumble's Dad after their deliberations.

"Dad, we will give you a special friends and family deal of... only... £18.75!"

The tension was palpable.

"You two scallywags! I'll take it!" and with a quick handshake the deal had been done.

Tumble's Dad tucked the painting under his arm and wandered off to meet a friend who wanted to discuss a "humanitarian" construction project of sorts.

Our two artists were handed £18.75, which they had trouble splitting between themselves.

After much fussing they decided to take their earnings and spend it on one of life's great luxuries, a hot chocolate, with cream and extra marshmallows.

They even had a fair bit left over, which Sassy put into his piggy bank at home for safe keeping, and which Tumble's mother made her son spend on buying new, clean, mittens.

The lost tale of Jackson the penguin farmer

One mans quest to make penguins happy

By Virginia W.

The acclaimed Noel Prize winning walrus sanctuary owner

✳ ✳ ✳ ✳ ✳ - "Very sincere " J.K. Reindeer

Many days had been spent saving the money for his little project. The penguins were put to bed, and he set to work on his masterpiece.

All night was spent mixing paints and putting brush to canvas. He knew that this could be his ticket to making his dream come true.

The painting was finished by morning. Jackson had got no sleep but was proud of his accomplishment. A local art collector had said he would pay a hefty price for a picture that encapsulated wonder, optimism and tragedy, something that Jackson knew plenty about. His penguins would finally be able to get that playground that they had always wanted. He imagined how happy their little faces would be when he told them the great news. Project Penguin Paradise was GO!

Jackson spent the day, as he usually did, petting his penguins and feeding them. He didn't want to tell them the news yet. It was going to be a little surprise.

The next day he got up early, before any of his little friends had awoken. He carefully put the painting on his skidoo and went into town.

The house of the Art Collector was easily found. It was made of marble columns that towered over all the other houses in the neighbourhood.

A butler, a little Penguin by the name of Williams, opened the door and told Jackson to set up the painting in the garden, by the canopy. Williams explained that the Art Buyer would be down shortly, he was just enjoying an early morning movie in his home cinema.

Not to worry, Jackson thought, and as he headed into the mansion's garden. He mused over inviting Williams, and his children, to the new playground once it was built.

That would be nice.

Jackson set up his easel in the garden, and put a big cloth over the painting in order not to ruin the surprise. He stood back quickly as he heard the Art Buyer coming down the stairs.

He calmed his nerves.

"Hello, my humble apologies for being late! WALRUSMAN, The Final Chapter, Part 4 is one of my favourite high budget independent motion pictures. I'm in a good mood. Let's see the painting now!" said the Art Buyer, with a flourish.

Jackson enthusiastically whipped off the cloth. It fell slowly. The Art Buyer's eyes sparkled.

"What a masterpiece! It is exactly what I had always envisioned. But it would take a real genius to create something so emotive, so raw. Jackson. You are that genius. I'll write a check for you at once!"

Suddenly, a snowball fell from the sky. It landed on the canopy with a dramatic thunk then bounced on to the painting with an almighty splat. The painting fell on Jackson, who in shock said "OW!?".

He wasn't really injured, but was hurt to see his work of art ruined. The paints had run together. The fabric had softened...

"Hmm. The weather really seems to have taken a turn for the worse! What with these recent snowball showers and all. What a disaster! I should really get a real conservatory built!" said the Art Buyer and went inside before more snowballs rained from the sky.

...

Williams showed Jackson to the door. On the way home, Jackson passed the local skip. He picked up his ruined painting and looked at it one last time. Maybe if he left it here, someone would pick it up. As long as it brought joy to someone, he thought, he would be happy.

He returned to his farm, fed and petted the penguins as usual, and went to bed.

Maybe he didn't need money to build the playground after all. All he needed was someone with tools and experience!

The dream could still come true! He would give his good friend Mr Tumble a call in the morning.

A thick fog fell across North Pole City on that fateful night. The moon was full, casting jagged shadows on the snow. A perfect night for a crime, and a particularly horrid crime at that...

<u>Morning: 9:03 School.</u>

"Children! Settle down now! Button! Tumble! Stop wrestling!"

"I've nearly got him Mrs Appleshine!" said Tumble, in mid-flight, with a waste paper basket on his head. His words were a little muffled.

"Children! NOW!" All pupils were seated at their place a mere instant later. Good as gold. Though Tumble still had old homework and chewing gum stuck to him.

"As you all know" continued Mrs Appleshine "Today is our yearly class election. In the running is the formidable Mr. Harvey Dolt! He has done a great job over the past couple of years, especially with his no-running-in-the-halls policy. Our other candidate, trying to clinch the position once again, is the enthusiastic Mr. Tumble... He wants to have a new compulsory-running-in-the-halls policy. Sadly, children, your votes from yesterday have been misplaced. I'll look for them at break time, so you'll not find out who has won till after then."

Everyone was terribly disappointed about the delay. Especially Tumble, who couldn't wait to run in the hallways.

The lesson continued as usual. Today they were practising their handwriting. Tumble got out his pencil case, unzipped it and shook out one chewed up yellow pencil. He borrowed a sharpener from Sassy. He liked the point to be super sharp. After having patiently sharpened the pencil to the perfect point, he noticed that there was nothing left but the rubber at the very end! He coyly asked Sassy whether he could borrow a pencil as well. It was a little bit blunt but it would have to do. He focused his attention, and began his first sentence. The lesson dragged on, and on, and on... After what had seemed like an eternity to Tumble, who had patiently finished off four and a half sentences, a crunched up paper ball landed on his desk. No one else seemed to have noticed. He picked it up slowly and unravelled it to find a message written inside.

"Not all is as it seems. Meet me in the playground. Poppy."

An adventure! Tumble was terribly excited, and worked hard till the end of the lesson, finishing off another two whole sentences.

Tumble saw Poppy across the playground and casually walked over to her. He then casually lent against the merry-go-round.

"Hey. What's going on Pops?" he asked cool as a bean.

"Tumble. There is a thief in our midst! Someone stole that envelope with our votes in it!"

"So maybe-Uhgg!" The merry-go-round lazily turned and Tumble's hand slipped off. "You. Ow. Want to play marbles with us?... Wait a minute! A Mystery?"

"Yes! Exactly! We need you and Sassy to find out who stole that envelope."

Tumble had done a bit of detective work in his spare time but this was going to be his biggest case to date. He was a professional though and didn't come cheap.

"I'll, of course, need to be paid. In chocolate naturally"

"Tumble! Fine. One milky bar to share between you two"

"Hmmm. A very tasty offer... One bar each or no deal"

"You'll get one and a half bars between you. Last offer!"

"Ok. But then we get the ones with nuts inside"

"Deal!"

They shook on it. Poppy explained that she had a witness lined up and that she would need them to talk to him.

Tumble told her not to worry. The case was in the best possible hands. She walked off confident in Tumble's great detective skills.

Tumble found Sassy and told him everything he knew, which wasn't a great deal really, and the two set off to talk to their first witness, Button McShane.

Sassy had read many detective books and knew of a scientific way of getting information out of a witness. Sassy would play a nice detective and Tumble a grumpy one. Tumble would surprise Button, maybe tell him that he had silly handwriting or something (he'd improvise). Then kind Sassy would come in. Button would trust the nice, compassionate, intelligent Sassy and then tell him everything he knew about the crime. It was a foolproof plan.

They nonchalantly approached Button.

"Watch this Sassy. I'll get him good!" Tumble wandered over to where Button was riding the school seesaw. Up and down, up and down. When Button had reached the highest point in his journey, Tumble leapt at him. Up, and unexpectedly sideways.

The two fell into the fresh snow and started wrestling. Sassy looked on. He had hoped for a more subtle approach. He watched as the two took it in turns to throw each other into the snow. After a good few minutes he thought it was time to play his part as the nice detective.

"Button. How you doing buddy?"

Button replied by flipping Tumble over his shoulder into the snow.

"You want a hand?"

Button jumped at Tumble, who Karate-dodged out of the way.

"Button! Where were you this morning, before class? Did you see anything suspicious?"

Tumble hopped onto Button.

"Button?"

Button wriggled free and tried to suplex Tumble.

"Tumble?"

After another few minutes of intense questioning the two wrestlers were out of breath. They had given up and decided to have a little lie down. They each lay in a little snow angel they had accidentally made during the struggle. Sassy went over to Tumble.

"He'll never talk," Sassy said.

"He's too well trained. There's nothing *phew* we can do." agreed Tumble panting breathlessly.

Maybe they should try to find some useful evidence instead of *wrestling* with people thought Sassy.

So off he went while Tumble had a short nap in his snow angel to recover his strength.

Sassy went looking for a magnifying glass from one of the school's science labs. He also found a hat that he thought was appropriate for a detective. He scoured the whole playground. No stone lay unturned. No crevasse unchecked. He finally stumbled on some evidence. It was a note, with a name on it. Tumble woke up and lazily crawled over.

"What have you found there?" he asked.

"It is a note! With the thief's name on it!" replied Sassy proudly.

"How do you know it is the thief's name?" inquired Tumble.

"Simple, my dear Tumble. At closer inspection with my magnifying glass we can see this…"

Sassy held the magnifying glass so that Tumble could see.

"The magnifying glass focuses light so that the object looks bigger," explained Sassy.

Tumble was impressed but not for long. For you see it was a bright summer's day and the sun's rays were focused straight at the crucial evidence.

It caught fire.

Sassy looked at the little heap of ash in the snow. "That wasn't supposed to happen."

"What did it say Sassy? What name was written on it?"

"I didn't have time to read it unfortunately."

"What a disaster. What are we going to do?" asked Tumble.

After a thoughtful pause Sassy answered, "We are going to ask witnesses to come forward. I have an idea."

Sassy explained the plan to Tumble. They went through the playground telling everyone that if they knew anything about the crime, they should meet them on the school roof in 5 or 10 minutes (or any time in between really).

The two detectives climbed up the fire escape ladder and waited patiently for the witnesses to flood in. No one came. The sun was beating down on them. And they waited and waited...

"They'll never come, the scaredy-cats," grumbled Tumble. His back was turned. A plume of cold breath reached into the sky.

Finally, after many agonising minutes, a figure emerged over the top of the fire escape ladder. It was Button.

"Hello Button. What's up?" asked Tumble

"Don't talk. I need to tell you something important before it's too late. Sorry I'm late, but I had to have a quick nap. I know who committed the crime..."

Tumble and Sassy were on the edge of their metaphorical seats.

"The person who committed the crime was..."

Button never finished his sentence, for he was silenced by the school bell. It rang suspiciously early. Mrs Appleshine was waving the children back inside. They would never get to hear what Button had to say.

The villain had won.

The School day continued as usual. No more evidence came to light. Mrs Appleshine finally found the envelope with the votes inside. Tumble had lost to Harvey again.

After school Tumble slowly sulked home by himself.

"Tumble, wait up!" it was Poppy.

"Hi, Poppy."

"I'm sorry that you didn't win, I hope you're not too upset. It's probably for the best though," explained Poppy sympathetically.

"You're right," answered Tumble "I was a symbol of hope but I would only have made things worse by giving my fellow pupils their freedom. Running in the corridors would be a hazard to all. How irresponsible of me."

He looked down at his feet pensively.

"I will resign my post as School Detective in the morning, Poppy. Harvey is what the school needs at this moment in time."

"You're right Tumble. See you in school on Monday. Oh, and just so you know, by the way. You got my vote."

Before Poppy scuttled off home, she placed something in Tumbles hand.

It was a milky bar.

And with that, Tumble the detective walked into the misty night, munching his milky bar, never to work another case again.

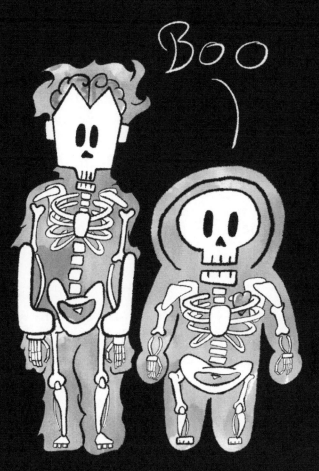

Poppy was spending the weekend at her grandparents' house on the outskirts of North Pole City. She had done all her homework and had learnt her new routine for the circus show, so she asked the boys over for a play date.

Sassy and Tumble arrived bright and early to make the most of the day. Gertrude, Poppy's grandmother, opened the door and everyone shuffled into the house. Sassy politely complimented a small patch of wallpaper to Gertrude's great delight and Tumble eagerly ran off to find Poppy.

The three spent a great deal of time catching up. Sassy told them how he had read a book on how to have a perfect memory but to everyone's disappointment he had forgotten what it was called.

Poppy showed them a scar she had picked up when training Leo the ferocious lion to do a dangerous new trick. She had tripped over a tightrope and grazed her knee. Leo reacted quickly though and brought her a first aid kit, so it really looked more like a bruise than a scar. She insisted that it could have been fatal though.

Tumble couldn't think of any stories to share with his friends, so he suggested they play hide and seek. They bloomin' loved hide and seek!

Sassy was counting (because he was the only one who could count proper) and the other two went off to hide.

"Where to hide?" whispered Tumble to himself. His eyes were frantically darting around the room desperately trying to find a suitable place.

"...Fourteen...Fifteen...Um..." Sassy was fast reaching the end of his countdown.

Tumble was running out of time. He suddenly had a great thought! At the last second he dashed out of the room, went straight up the stairs into Poppy's bedroom and hid in her walk-in closet.

"Ready or not, here I come!"

Sassy quickly found a contorted Poppy hidden in a laundry basket and together they went off to find Tumble. But try as they might, he was nowhere to be found.

After many minutes of searching the house, Gertrude invited the kids into the kitchen for some nice cold ice-cold smoothies.

Poppy had one, and Sassy had two because he was bigger than Poppy of course.

"Aargh! Brain Freeze!" whined Sassy.

Serves him right! Thought Poppy.

Sassy felt better after a couple of moments though, so they resumed their conversation about what the best types of smoothies were.

They both loved smoothies...

Meanwhile Tumble was still hidden upstairs. He marvelled at how good he was at hiding. Maybe he could do this for a living one day. He was quiet as a mouse...

After finishing their smoothies, Sassy and Poppy watched a couple of hour's worth of old Duke Danger episodes. They finished the episode called "Duke Dukes it out with Dracula" and were now busy drawing mythical monsters.

Sassy came up with the names and Poppy drew them.

Some of Sassy's better names were as follows. A Ra-Spoon: a half Racoon, half spoon. An Ali-Frator: a crocodile freight train hybrid. And finally, a Hedge-log. He didn't really know what that was a mixture of but it sounded ferocious.

Poppy didn't think that any of these creatures seemed very dangerous though, but Sassy had saved his best for last.

"Are you ready Poppy? This is a good one. Ready? It's called... A sea-lion! Like a lion but it lives... in the sea! Geddit? Do you geddit, Poppy? Poppy? You geddit? Poppy..."

Poppy did 'get it' and she loved it.

It reminded her of her little pet monster, Leo.

She drew a half lion, with tiger stripes, cheetah paws, a puma's tail, the roar of a really big Jaguar and for good measure she threw in a bit of cat.

It was perfect! All it needed now was colouring to make it look really lifelike.

"Wait here Sassy, I'll quickly nip upstairs and get my water colours from my room. I'll be right back."

She bolted upstairs, went into her room and brought out her chest with all of her art supplies...

Tumble, having had his eye eagerly glued to the closet's keyhole the whole time saw her rush in. He was terribly excited! He could hardly contain himself. Poppy brought the chest over to where Tumble was hiding. Tumble covered his mouth with his mittens to stop himself from making any sounds. He watched as Poppy put her chest back under her bed. He couldn't hold it in any longer! Poppy heard a muffled "Pffffteehheehhe" sound from her closet and turned in fright. She had always suspected that her closet was a bit haunted. She shivered with fear and screamed.

Sassy heard the scream and stopped trying to come up with a clever name for a half-monkey half-wrench monster beast. He ran up the stairs and saw Poppy frozen to the spot.

"What is it Poppy!?"

She couldn't speak. All she could do was point a trembling hand at her closet, which in response made a spooky "Tschprrrrthihihi" sound.

Sassy looked in disbelief. He earnestly put a hand on Poppy's shoulder and said, "Oh my. Poppy. You have a ghost in your closet."

Poppy calmed down a bit after Sassy explained that he was knowledgeable in 'paranormal infestigations' and would have that ghost out in no time. He just had to talk it into leaving the house. In preparation he quickly had one last smoothie, and began his ghost expulsion routine.

"Oh great ghost. What is your name and purpose for haunting Poppy's walk-in closet?" asked Sassy, hands raised high above his head.

After a short pause a muffled "Muhahahaha" came from the door. Very spooky. Sassy hid behind Poppy, who then in turn quickly hid behind Sassy.

Sassy continued in a stammer "Would y-you please kindly l-leave us alone... p...p....puh.... please."

There was no answer. Just the muffled sound of someone straining to hold in a fart.

Sassy had an idea. He would have to confront the ghost in person. He got a rope, tied it around his waist and got Poppy to hold the other end.

"Poppy. I'm going in. I will enter the Ghost Dimension. This is one small step for me but one ma-hooo-ssive step for human ghost relations. You have to pull me out when you feel me tug at the rope. If I don't make it back Poppy, promise that you will look after my cat, King Cole."

"Sassy, you are ever so brave!" This was a new look for Sassy. He preferred to be the brains in the group. Where was Tumble when you really needed him?

Poppy ran over to Sassy, and gave him a quick hug. One lonely little tear crept down her cheek.

"Go get 'em you... you Ghost Annihilator!"

"Start tonight's episode of Duke Danger without me Pops. I'll be right back."

He slowly opened the door. A thin beam of light crept into the closet. He walked in cautiously. This was a completely alien world. Ugly hooks hung everywhere. Ghoulish fabrics billowed in the cold breeze. He inched forward.

There, in the shadows, was a figure. The light fell on the ghostly shape and what he saw next chilled him to the bone.

It was a small pale ugly misshapen monster-boy thing.

Sassy gave a shrill scream. The ghost gave a manic laugh.

Its eyes were filled with madness.

Poppy tugged the rope as hard as she could. Sassy practically flew out of the closet, grabbed Poppy and ran down the stairs.

Tumble was a bit confused. Weren't they supposed to find him?

He went downstairs, where Poppy and Sassy were cowering behind the sofa. He popped his head over the back of the couch and asked what was going on. They were both a little surprised to see him after his lengthy absence. But there was no time to ask Tumble what he had been up to. There was a ghost in the house after all!

Poppy explained the whole story. Tumble listened intently.

After Poppy finished her gruesome tale, they all looked at each other, pale as – well – ghosts.

"I think, we should stay here, behind the sofa, just in case that monster boy is still upstairs," said Tumble.

They all agreed that that was the best thing to do.

The three stayed huddled together for the rest of the day till Tumble's Mum came to pick the boys up.

In the car back home Tumble's Mum asked whether the boys had behaved themselves and played outside in the fresh air.

They looked at each other and hesitantly said, "Yes".

Tumble's Mum was not ready for this story. They would have to keep it as their secret for a while still.

In fact, Poppy, Tumble and Sassy never spoke of the incident again... The secret was lost forever...

Until now!

Dear reader. You have discovered 'THE EXCELLENT ADVENTURES OF SASSY & TUMBLE'.

Now you too know the secret.

Don't tell anyone though.

Promise...

"Tumble! It's about to start!"

Sassy was already on the sofa, eagerly awaiting the latest adventure of Duke Danger on the television. Tumble hurried into the room with a bowl of popcorn and two cups of frothy hot chocolate.

"Here you go Sassy. Your 'cold chocolate'. They both looked at each other and sniggered because the chocolate was in fact hot, not cold. Not even lukewarm, or would have been if it hadn't already spilt on the carpet. This was all part of the weekly Duke Danger ritual.

"It was great last week when Duke crash landed on Mount Everest, and built that snow mobile out of the wreckage," said Sassy.

"What an inspiration," agreed Tumble.

The title sequence started to play. Our two adventurers sang along. They knew every single one of the words.

"Duke Danger, Duke Danger! Danger is his middle name! He travels the world. Has been to both poles. La-di-da-da, Adventure finds him. He always seems to win. The evil guys always end up in the, bin! DUKE DANGERRR!!!" they shouted the last part as loud as they could. Tumble's Mum popped her head in to see if everything was all right.

The title music faded and the episode started.

"Don't you think it's weird that he has never been to North Pole City, Tumble?"

"Shhhhhhh! Look, he's in the jungles of Peru or maybe Bolivia!"

The Duke was cutting a path through black and white ferns. When he stumbled into a clearing, where there stood a huge lion.

Duke said: "I'm not *lion* when I say that we are going to have a *wild* time my friend!! It's going to get *hairy*!"

After a pensive moment Sassy and Tumble both laughed fanatically, slapping knees and sending popcorn flying everywhere. Good old Duke always knew how to make an entrance.

"I'm going to grow up just like him," said Tumble. (Damn, should have said, "growl up like him!").

"You've got a lot of growing to do Tumble. Teeeheeeheee"

"Oi! Hahaha... on the TV he's only this big you know"

Tumble, with arm outstretched and thumb in air tried to cover the Duke on the TV screen. His thumb barely covered The Duke's square chin. The now legendary moustache appeared to sprout from his mitten like powerful wings. Tumble thought that maybe he too should grow a moustache.

"Watch out Duke!!! Behind you!!! Phew, I really thought he was going to be crushed to death by that boulder!" exclaimed Sassy in one quick breath.

Tumble's thumb didn't even cover the boulder. Maybe his other thumb would fare better.

"Hmmmmmmm. Sassy... I just had a strange thought"

"That was close!!! Man, he has super reflexes!"

"So, Sassy..." Sassy turned to listen, "Don't you think it's a bit strange that... The Duke goes on exactly one adventure a week, and always on a Sunday?"

"Well Tumble, I guess it just fits in with his schedule, you know. Even well practiced adventurers like us don't have an adventure *every* day... He needs time to watch TV like everyone else in his down time, you know, in between saving Fräulein Doris. He needs time to book flights and eat and stuff..."

"I guess you're right Sassy... but... doesn't it strike you as a little odd that Fräulein Doris always gets kidnapped on a Sunday too. You can't really plan to be kidnapped... can you?"

"Well... Tumble, she might get kidnapped on the Saturday or the Friday, and Duke Danger only finds out on the Sunday between 6:30 and 7:00 o'clock."

That was also true, thought Tumble. Did Saturday come before Sunday? He'd look that one up later instead of asking Sassy.

This week Fräulein Doris had been kidnapped by a tribe of jungle people. After having been bitten by a snake and having to suck the poison out, The Duke made it his mission to save her. Tumble took a sip from his hot chocolatey Duke Danger cup.

"It's very clever how he made that parachute out of tree bark," observed Sassy, who always kept mental notes of the Duke's inventions in case they ever came in handy on one of his own expeditions.

The Duke had ambushed the jungle tribe, and with two precise shots from his revolver freed Fräulein Doris from her shackles.

"Whoa! Did you see that Sassy!"

"I can't believe my eyes!"

"Absolutely great! I'm not half as accurate with my bow and arrow."

"That was soooo WICKED!" Sassy snapped his fingers.

"Wicked? Um. Sassy? Are you ok?"

"Yea. Sorry Tumble. I don't know what came over me. It's just so exciting…"

The two boys munched popcorn and watched Duke Danger. A few stupendous minutes later Tumble turned to Sassy again and asked.

"You know school sort of gets in the way of having fun, and in school we get homework, which stops us from having fun outside of school... How did Duke ever find time to become an adventurer?"

"That's a very smart point. I reckon Danger never went to school, so I guess that's how he has always had time to do fun things. Like beat up that crocodile in 'Swamp Madness'."

"Remember that episode called 'School of Schlock'?" asked Tumble.

"Yea, 'course. It's one of my favourites. How could I forget?"

"Well he was in school then."

"Oh yeah. I guess he was, wasn't he?"

...

The episode ended a short while later. The two boys agreed that that had been the best episode yet so Sassy went home.

"See you in school tomorrow!" he said over his shoulder and hummed the Duke Danger theme to himself as he headed out into the snow.

Tumble brushed his teeth and went to bed. He dreamed about growing up just like Duke Danger, saving people in exotic countries and being famous.

He would work doubly hard in school from now on, he thought. If he got good grades, maybe he could go to university and study adventuring one day, and get one of those square hats with a tassel on a string that students wore.

He would wake up bright and early to get all of tomorrow's homework done.

Just like the Duke...

He knew he wasn't really like the Duke but a hot chocolate moustache was a little bit like a real moustache, he thought to himself as he drifted off to sleep.

"So we have learnt that if we take 5 away from 2, we get a negative number," Mrs Appleshine was lazily writing on the chalkboard. "Do you understand Sassy?"

The rest of the class had already dozed off. Sassy stroked his chin thoughtfully.

"If my calculations are correct. I believe that this goes against the laws of the universe. I read a book on it once. 'Cooking for Dummies 101'. It's what they teach at university. No, really. I cannot have a cake, and eat it"...

"Without getting fat! Hahaha!" interrupted Tumble cheerily.

The whole class woke up and as one they laughed and laughed and then dozed off again. Tumble's head hit the edge of the table with a little thud.

"...and still have a cake left over at the end, just crumbs," finished Sassy.

"Sassy, a cake is not quite like a number", said Mrs Appleshine with gentle confusion.

"I understand, Mrs Appleshine," said Sassy. He didn't really. "Numbers are like... um... maths problems and cakes are like... um... pastries or treats"

Fig: The crucial step to understanding cakes:

(Remember to whisk the eggs)

The school bell rang and Mrs Appleshine quickly cleaned the scribbles on the chalkboard and practically ran out of the door. The other children followed suit.

The schoolyard was where Tumble, Sassy and all their friends had some of their best adventures. Today, they were playing football.

Little Tumble was in goal but was quickly replaced by Sassy.

Button blew his whistle and the game was on.

It was a great game, legendary in fact. Button and Tumble were head to head running for the ball. The score was 0-0 as usual. Button kicked the ball as hard as he could. It flew straight at Sassy who with a swift Kung-Fu kick deflected it to the side. The ball then bounced off the window of Principal Dimly's office and straight into Poppy's little face. She fell backward into a pile of snow.

"Ow!" said Poppy "That hurt,"

Everyone crowded around Poppy. Button took a stick and poked at her.

"I think she's dead... we'll need a new player to replace her," he said.

"Leave me alone Button," said Poppy. Button was as silly as always. "I'm not dead!"

"I'm so sorry Poppy," apologised Sassy. "Are you okay?"

"Yeah it's ok, normally you never save a ball, tee-hee-hee." (Sassy's Kung-Fu skills had tremendously improved since he stopped using that blindfold.)

It was obvious that Poppy needed medical attention. Brave Tumble mustered up all his courage, knelt next to Poppy and said, "No, Poppy, don't stand, you'll only make it worse for yourself, soooo, much, worse..."

Poppy hopped to her feet. "No Tumble, I'm fine..."

Tumble urgently turned to the huddle of primary school children.

"Is there a doctor present? It's an emergency! No one... Fine, I, Dr. Tumble MD have all the first aid training and will save your life Poppy!"

First things first.

"Button, you get hot chocolate. Button? NOW! Sassy, make a stretcher... use your imagination! We don't have time! I will perform the life saving manoeuvre now... Clear!!!"

He knew exactly what he was doing. Before Poppy could protest, Tumble gave her the biggest "life saving" hug he could muster. That would buy them a bit of time...

"Um, thank you Tumble. Do you mind not squeezing me quite so hard?" Poppy squeaked.

Sassy had made a stretcher from the football goal posts and net and gave it to Tumble.

"Just in the nick of time!" said Tumble, "Guys, let's go get the patient some hot chocolate!"

They all helped the 'helpless' Poppy onto the stretcher and Sassy and Tumble lifted her up into the air. On reflection Poppy thought she could get used to this. It was pretty fun being carried around.

"It's like I'm a shark caught in a net. But a shark that likes hot chocolate and is a vegetarian! Woohooooo!!!"

"Hang in there!" said Sassy. Tumble, the stretcher, Poppy and finally Sassy all headed up the hill towards school.

"Faster, Tumble, we need to go faster! I think we're loosing her!"

"Sassy, my little legs are going as fast as they can!"

"Faster!!!"

"Nooooooooooo!"

"Help!" said Poppy, as she flopped around on her makeshift stretcher.

Tumble's legs were a blur. He could do it! He had to run faster if he was going to save his friends life. The stairs to the school were coming up fast. He needed to synchronise his feet to coincide with the steps perfectly so as not to fall. He would have to bend his knees to compensate for the gradient of the stairs and place his feet firmly on -

Clumsily, he tripped right before he reached the first step. He face-planted into the snow. The stretcher lodged in the ground and Poppy was catapulted right out of it.

She went flying!

Poppy bounced right off the Principal's window and rolled straight back down the hill from whence she came.

"Help!" yelped Poppy again and with an almighty crash hit one of the school's ice sculptures, finally coming to rest.

The abstract piece of art shattered! Shards of ice went all over the place. Whatever it was in the first place was now destroyed! Poppy was covered in ice and snow and now had a runny nose and was cold and a bit fed up.

Poor Poppy took the rest of the day off school to recover from her accident. Tumble and Sassy thought about what they could do to cheer her up. They decided to write her a comforting letter.

It went a little like this:

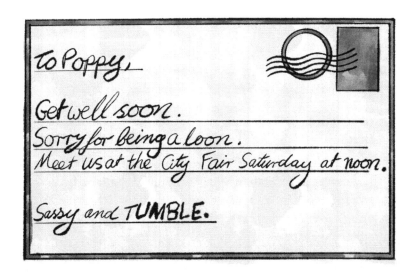

To Poppy,
Get well soon.
Sorry for being a loon.
Meet us at the City Fair Saturday at noon.

Sassy and TUMBLE.

They hoped it wasn't too formal. Plus Sassy claimed that rhymes had healing properties. So that was good.

...

Saturday rolled around and our two buddies went to the fair.

There were huge balloons, confetti, music and good humour all around. After a short while Tumble started worrying. He wasn't sure that Poppy would turn up! Maybe she had gotten lost?

"Where is she?" asked Tumble impatiently.

Sassy was munching on a great big wad of candyfloss and without stopping said "*munch* don't worry, she'll be here somewhere *munch*. We gave her plenty of hot chocolate so there's no chance she's deceased from her *munch* lacerations."

Time passed. Very slowly. Finally a little voice behind Tumble said "Hi Tumble. Hi Sassy. We were looking all over for you guys". It was Poppy and her best friend Moin-Moin.

"Well as well as being, um, clever and funny, my camouflage talents are also great. Second-to-none in fact. So it's no real wonder you didn't see us immediately" said Tumble with perfect integrity.

"Once Tumble hid from a scary penguin by disguising himself as a tiny pile of snow," laughed Sassy.

"I only hid because then I could ambush it, like this." Tumble started demonstrating his technique by tackling Sassy, who didn't much mind.

"And after I caught it I taught it many great tricks and it taught me how to talk to penguins in their 'sign talk' language, which is difficult to learn because they have flippers and we have thumbs." Tumble said proudly.

Poppy and Moin-Moin seemed impressed by Sassy, who during Tumble's feral attack, did not budge or stop munching his candy floss. Tumble finally gave up wrestling Sassy. By this time the parade was in full swing and he thought he had gotten his point across. They all gazed at a procession of huge mechanical animals, followed by ice skaters who swished and pirouetted along the road, leaving marks in the ice. Tumble had a great idea on how he could apologise to Poppy for their accident.

"Poppy?" Tumble asked.

"Yep?" she replied.

"Could I get you one of those small-ish balloons? Because we nearly killed you and all..."

"Oh please, that would be great! Yeah, I still can't feel my left pinkie toe. Look." She demonstrated the numbness of her toe by very gently kicking a lamp post.

"Absolutely nothing. It may never feel again..." she looked longingly at her left foot.

Tumble felt terrible. A balloon merchant was walking by and Tumble ran after him.

"Excuse me sir, could I buy a balloon from you please?" asked Tumble.

"Of course, what colour would you like?" Hmmm, what colour would Poppy want. Red. Maybe blue? It could even possibly be yellow? Or not a prime colour at all? Maybe one of those weird ones like purple... He bet that Sassy in his infinite wisdom would know which colour she would want.

Tumble was going to have to be brave and trust his instinct on this one.

Tumble got out his wallet and counted out his pocket money.

"Could I have a red one please?"

"Of course, here you go. And be careful not to float off little man" The vendor chuckled and walked on.

Tumble returned to his friends.

"Here Poppy I got you a red one, because red is the colour of... nice things like... daffodils!"

That was some quick thinking thought Tumble. He really was smart.

"Thank you Tumble", said Poppy (whose favourite colour was indeed red but knew that daffodils weren't really red at all. She knew Tumble was trying hard though and didn't mention it).

She beamed a friendly smile across her entirely freckled face. Before Tumble could explain that his many interests included flowers, of all colours and of all shapes, Moin-Moin's parents were calling the two girls over.

"I have to go. Sorry. We're going to the penguin farm for the day. I'll see you in school on Monday. OK? Bye-bye. Thank you for the balloon!" said Poppy and gave Tumble and Sassy a hug before running off after Moin-Moin.

Tumble turned slowly. He was a wise old man in a young boy's body. He really was just that. A sensei. Or samurai.

"Sassy," said the mystified Tumble. "We have been on many great adventures together, you and I, but that was by far the best one yet"

"I think you might be right. It was also pretty periloose, pearlyooz... peri... um...dangerous!" added Sassy "given that you nearly floated away and all".

They both giggled childishly.

So our two brave heroes talked about their adventures together and what might lie ahead for them.

Sassy was sure that red was the right colour to choose for a girl called Poppy, just over fluorescent orange of course. However he knew that daffodils were not actually red. They were yellow.

But Tumble seemed so happy.

He didn't want to spoil the moment, so he kept that as his little secret...

THE END

Sassy and Tumble will be back...

Dearest Reader,

Thank you for joining in on the adventure.

If you would like to show your support, leaving an honest review online helps out massively.

Hopefully you enjoyed yourself and I wish you the best of luck in any epic little quests that you may embark on in the future.

Kindest regards,

Ben

P.S.

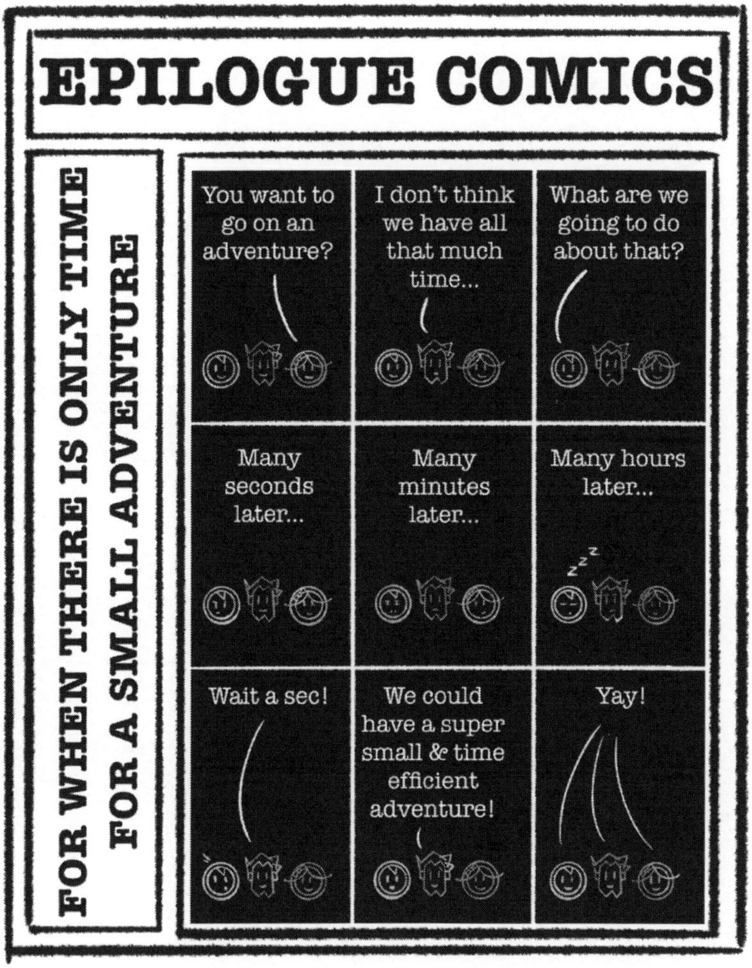
EPILOGUE COMICS
FOR WHEN THERE IS ONLY TIME FOR A SMALL ADVENTURE
You want to go on an adventure?
I don't think we have all that much time...
What are we going to do about that?
Many seconds later...
Many minutes later...
Many hours later...
Wait a sec!
We could have a super small & time efficient adventure!
Yay!

OK. I'm going to have to...

...hit that trampoline perfectly...

...for a soft landing

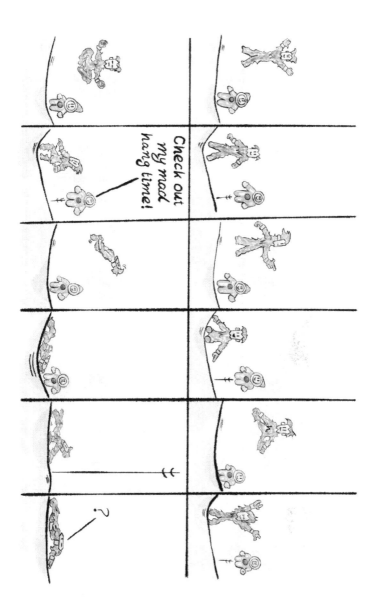

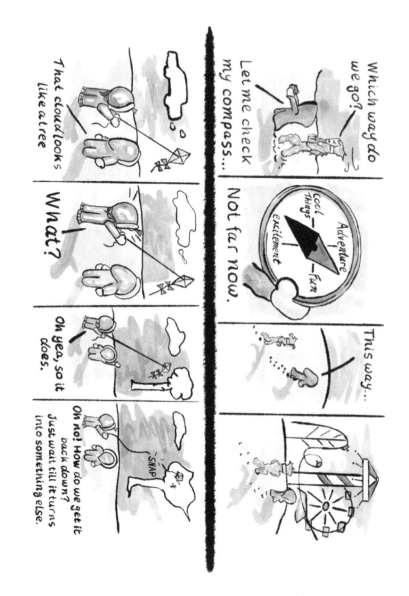

Leo, Sit!

Leo, Roll over

Well done! You're so clever

Also, could you help me with my homework?

Rock, Paper, Scissors!

HAHA! I win again!

You always go rock!

It's just, I find it difficult to make anything but a rock...

Printed in Great Britain
by Amazon